Editors Word

By Edna J. White, editor, Author Life Coach & Speaker

Life had just stopped, like so many I have been mostly confined to my apartment. People on the outside stockpiling toilet paper and hand sanitizer without other hygiene products or items, still confuse me.

Then in a fit of inspiration, I started my list of what positive things I can add to my day to fill the void of not socializing personally. Only to find out it was harder than I realized. The one thing I kept hearing is wash your hands, not like mom never told us that. Even when we came to the dinner table after a shower, she woud scream out "go wash your hands". It's a wonder why our skin was still attached. I digress.

In mind of this pandemic, I want to encourage you all to keep your NOW side. With the coronavirus reminding people of the importance of basic hygiene now, and staying home, now all the while shoving news reports of all the bad down our throats and feeding our horror, keep inspired. There will be death as it is part of life just as there are two sides of happiness.

Living in the now means **living life** with more joy and enthusiasm. The present moment **is the** only moment in our **lives** that you actually have. The pandemic showed us that by shutting down present business as well as future events. We all are in a holding pattern to learn the significance of one another.

You see we've drummed up so much hatred in the past years of what we hate about ourselves, what we hate about the life we ask for, what we hate about the life we are given and do nothing with, what we hate about people, places and things… oh my! We forgot about it being in the right now!

 One could say when we are in the Now, we are either in a thoughtless state, abiding in Pure consciousness or Presence, or we are consciously thinking or doing something (but only that which is really needed for that moment). That thinking or doing is not redundant, but fully conscious and purposeful.

The perfect NOW response to every situation comes only from the state of Presence. That response can be pro-active or non-active. Living in the present gradually liberates us from all unnecessary burdens and allows us to live in the most efficient, yet peaceful way.

Many have said to me "easier said than done" and I would respond easier said for me to live in peace instead of pieces.

So as we gather at the bonds of our joined sinks let's sing "Happy Birthday" (twice!) soap up and live in the NOW to be at peace even in the wake of adversity. As most have said already "we are not alone".

Contact for Life Coaching or Speaking Engagements at:
Email: ednajwhite11@gmail.com
Website: https://msedna12.wixsite.com/ednawhitecoaching
Facebook: https://www.facebook.com/EJWCoaching/

The Featured Cover Artist

Facebook: Art of Tony Green
Instagram: tonygreenart
Website: www.tonygreenart. com
Contacts: +256700969173 /+256786969173

Born 18th October 1992 in Kampala Uganda, Tumusiime Tony aka Tony Green is a self-taught artist with a foundation course in Architecture at Kyambogo University in Kampala.

From as early as I could remember, I have always been an emotional and highly sensitive individual, inspired, touched and captivated by almost everything in my immediate surroundings. Around the age of 9, I vividly remember having a love and strong passion for drawing and painting. I found the instrument to be a humble one and I would often use the expression "aliveness" to describe it's technical and sentimental value. What fascinated me most about painting is that I could create tones and textures so defined and so abstract, an illusion of color would be formed before me. I became heavily inspired by this notion and spent most of my early years trying to utilize its technical use.

My work captures intimate moments and gives a glimpse of an inner private world, providing a window to our own introspective thoughts and our mystery. Therefore, I create paintings of personal struggle and intimate emotion. All the way I have discovered that we all share these feelings.

Painting for me is a means to explore the deeper meaning of life. Through painting, I seek to uncover the untold to reveal the invisible. I try to catch a glimpse of the inner soul of subjects like meditation.

I hope to take those who follow and see my works on a mystical journey to another universe. A spiritual world, where one can connect with nature and find strength and harmony within oneself.

I have an urge to understand how the elements work together and how we as people are affected by them. I tend to create imagery with a "darker feel" to shed light on mysteries that are unknown to us. Human beings are pattern recognizers and as such we see things that are not always there. We prescribe meanings to natural phenomena that often don't carry any.

Therefore, I use the elements in my works to open them up to viewer's interpretations.

NJOVU (AFRICAN ELEPHANT)
Acryics on canvas
120cm*180cm

MOUNTAIN GORILLA
Acrylics on canvas
80cm*80cm

DEPTH OF HYPOCRISY
Acrylics on canvas
64cm*64cm

MPOLOGOMA (LION)
Acrylics on canvas
62cm*62cm

ABANDONED MOTHER
Acrylics on canvas
100cm*78cm

Life is Living and Dying

Howard Lee II Email: howard.leeiii89@gmail.com

StoryBook Poet StoryBook Enterprises LLC Poetry. Publishing. Radio

In life we live and then we die. Those words have many mixed emotions towards them as though we don't understand that we cannot have one without the other. If you live then you're guaranteed to die. This is not sad it is actually empowering because if we stop being so emotional about the subject we will understand that we must plant better seeds and accomplish great tasks in order to leave the next generations a foundation built on rock and not sand.

See we can make all the excuses: My parents weren't around, I'm a single parent, I went to jail, I'm at a job that isn't where I want to be, society etc. however, there is no benefit to not walking or living out your plan or purpose. Why would you quit or think minimal of yourself then expect anyone to love you more than you love yourself. I love the people and it is time we turn back to loving ourselves not in envy or pride. It is more about respectful and honorable love that will keep us away from the victim mindset. Yes, have things happened to you? You're still alive and you're living and you've probably overcome but you're so comfortable with your "story" because it is a way to make an excuse if you get called out for not reaching your potential.

Listen my family I believe in reaching our goals because if we line up just think how many others will line up. Believe that your life matters because it does and know that many people are connected to you saying yes and breaking through. I just sit and think of the progression in my life because many people said yes which made them available when I was coming through. They made themselves available and allowed me to build upon what they created. I get excited writing like this because yes it is exact and calling you out.

However, you need and need it. This type of love is true love because why would someone want to see you not living out your purpose when you are more than well capable, this is true love right here. I need you to stand up and shake off the hindrances. I need you to live free and on purpose. I end with this message, You only die with two things: who you were and who you've become and who you've become needs to be better than who you were.

"The fear of death
follows from the fear
of life. A man who lives
fully is prepared to die
at any time."

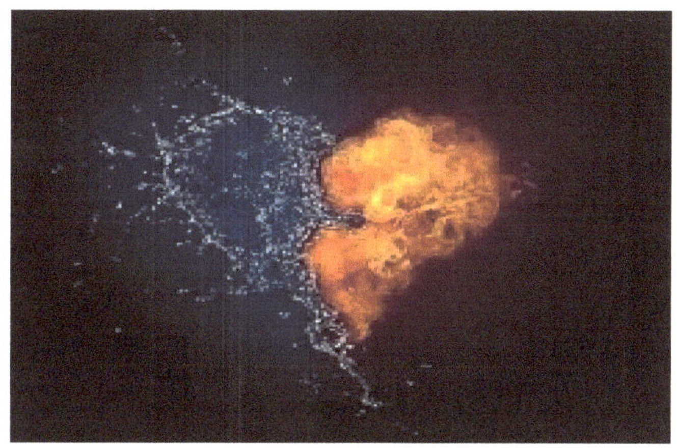

I was born for love
Despite the scars and wounds
The piercing words that have cut my soul
The negative energy that left me limping and crawling sometimes
The tears I cried brought up by People I trusted most.
Betrayals that I got laid in thought of comfort
Kisses that tasted like chocolate yet venom

Even If a downpour of hell floods my life
I will never give up on me
I will trust and love deeply again
My heart has been butchered to no life
But my courage resurrects it
Because I was born for Love

Am a spirit filled being that makes me special
I can overcome any negative energy
I can give joy and hope to the hopeless
I was born to love and live for love

By Athieno Catherine
Email: cathyathieno81@gmail.com
Tel: 256779542322

The Conscious Switch

Let me ask you a question, "Is pain and suffering a natural part of life to you?" Some of you may say yes, and some of you may say no, and depending on which chapter of my life you entered I'd be inclined to agree with both positions. In my mindless state I'd tell you pain, and suffering were two concepts that went hand in hand – both which rendered us powerless. In my mindful state I'd have to say pain is inevitable and suffering is a choice.

In a state of mindlessness everywhere I turned, I seemed to be surrounded by pain and suffering. In a nutshell pain was constantly showing up in different forms in my life, and I had grown a little tired of it – mentally I felt powerless over pain. I found myself navigating my life minding my own business and then boom out of nowhere, it seemed, pain and suffering would come along; like it had an open invitation to my life. Running away from pain didn't seem like an option, I tried to no avail. Avoiding daunting conversations with people – you know who I'm talking about and switching off shows that glorified pain and suffering. You name it I tried it. It seemed I couldn't escape it. The question lingered.

Why did pain seem to consume me internally? The past teaches me that I can survive the feeling and that I can also detach myself from the feeling. Sitting with the feelings also brings the revelation of the wisdom so I can grow.

Feelings just want to be felt. Mindfulness teaches me to show myself compassion even when I'm not comfortable. Showing compassion to the part of me that is struggling with stopping, the part of me that is judgmental, compassion for the pain. The conscious switch happens as I take a deep breath in right now to write these words to you in a way that makes sense and connects with where you are. Releasing myself from judgment of using just the right words to say just the right thing to convey my message and instead choosing to just be authentic with you letting my thoughts and feelings flow freely.

I want you to imagine that you and I are sitting, standing, lying down, or whatever just being together at this moment. Being here in the moment holding the space for what shows up right now. Wherever here is mentally, physically, spiritually, and emotionally. I want you to know that even though we are not physically together – I am here for you. I send my heart and energy of compassion as I write these words that pass through your consciousness as you read. Knowing that even here right now we can stop and connect with a state of peace using the power of our breath and our conscious awareness. So, go ahead take a moment to stop and breathe with me.

Never get it done. We are always practitioners never getting it right indefinitely, so it's

important to take a moment to stop. Tomorrow is always presenting us with a better way to understand the lessons we live – we can't
do it all today, so there is no reason to try. Not taking a moment to stop and reflect is often the source of our suffering.

Tomorrow or three months from now, I will review this literary piece and realize there is something I forgot to say, a better way I could have relayed my intention with this piece – no matter how much time I spend on it this will be my state of mind tomorrow if I live in a state of mindless suffering. So, I might as well make peace with whatever I can share now and let it go – switching to a state of mindfulness which teaches us that the gift of learning lessons is never done.

I can choose to suffer, regretting, wishing, hoping or I can take the lessons and use it to write again tomorrow from a place of growth and wisdom. As I study mindfulness intellectually and in my everyday life and practice, I see that all pain and suffering come from the seed of what I just shared – the power of our choices and where we place our attention. We are here making choices to learn and grow from not to hold ourselves in imprisonment of how the choices did or didn't pan out.

We can use mindfulness to make The Conscious Switch. The ability to take your mind off the things that are causing you pain is one of the gifts a mindfulness practice offers. As you bring your complete attention to aligning your thoughts with your breath you find a sense of unconditional peace. A peace that is not contingent on you completely understanding the conditions of your life right now, a peace that can exist even during pain, when things aren't all worked out and when you don't know what tomorrow may bring. Because the truth is all we have is the present moment and most times, if we are not practicing mindfulness, we miss the present moment all together.

The solutions to help us end suffering from the pain we encounter could be right in front of us.

So, let's stop. Take a conscious switch by inhaling with me now, allow the breath to flow in a rhythmic way expanding the belly on the inhale and then release out of your mouth hollowing out the belly on the exhale.

Make the Conscious Switch and keep doing so until you feel an unconditional shift to peace.

April Diane
Integrative Nutrition Health Coach

Chesapeake Bay

Oh where, oh where are you Chesapeake Bay?
How far away are you to my okay?
More mundane Monday's my day to play
Few fun day Friday's my weak payday
Oh where for art thou golden shore?
How's my heart glow embolden more?
Tis torn apart forever more
Once was a sinner, once was a whore
Until I stood up and said NO MORE!
Where did you sleep, my sandy beach?
How are you still so out of reach?
Sunrise hazing catching my peace
Sky rise living attracting beasts
All that I want is a peaceful beast
Cuz I'm convinced mankind's a beast
Just to be invincible to their bite
I had to love myself day and night
I had to make myself learned and bright
Where if you dare are you my dark knight?
How long until I am your delight?
Chesapeake Bay you're still out of sight
I'll see you soon under an April moon
I'll feel your motion and I will be moved
I'm bursting out of this old cocoon soon
Walking your beaches, I will be consumed
Where is my karma, how goes my mood?

Chesapeake Bay you're my good attitude

Our Feature Back Cover Artist

By Jennene Christine Obremski, a survivor or child physical, sexual and emotional abuse as well as rape and religious sexual abuse. For this poet and artist she finds healing and distraction from her blues. She donates part of the proceeds from the art found on shopvida.com/collections/jennene-christine-obremski?_ga to an orphanage in Kampala, Uganda and the U.S. supplying orphan girls with hygiene products and toiletries.

Here's Tejas

By Tejas Mathai
Tejasmathai.com

Hi, this is Tejas. I am a fourteen-year-old freshman living in Modesto, California. I am an author of two published sci-fi novels, Infinity: The Secret of the Diamonds and Infinity: The Rise of the Mandroids. I have been writing stories ever since I was six years old. This is my second article for Speak Magazine, and I am excited to contribute to this edition.

Since my first article for this magazine, I have made much progress on my writings. After the completion of my second book, I immediately began to work on my third book in the series. And in January of this year, I completed the first draft for my third book.

Outside of my writing, I also earned my Red 1 belt for karate.

In February. I am very excited to share my feature conversation with Dr. Nivedita Lakhera, who I met in San Jose, California. Dr. Lakhera, or Niv, as she prefers to be called, works as a physician at O'Connor Hospital in San Jose. She is a leader in contemporary poetry and an advocate for gender equality and human rights.

She is an award-winning author of two poetry and art books. Her first book, Pillow of Dreams, is an award-winning and best reviewed poetry book on Amazon for three consecutive years. Her second book, I am Not a Princess, I am a Complete Fairytale, has been included in the syllabus of Peace and Justice at Michigan State and Wayne State Universities.

Here is the interview:

____

Tejas: Hey everybody, today I will be interviewing Dr. Niv Lakhera. She is a poet and an author of two best-selling poetry books on Amazon, and I will be asking her a couple of questions, so would you like to tell us more about yourself?

Niv: Hi everybody, I'm Niv, and I'm with the amazing science writer, who has written two books already. How old are you?

Tejas: Fourteen

Niv: By the time he's fourteen, he has written two books, I mean…yeah, but he is interviewing me. So yes, I have written two books. I'm a full-time physician, full-time writer, full-time foodie, full-time fashionista, full-time friend, full-time…sleep-lover, what not.

Tejas: So, my first question for you is "what inspired you to write?"

Niv: So, I cannot not write. I think we all are here for a purpose. We are designed to do certain things in this lifetime, and when we do those things, it makes us very transcendental and it's a different kind of high. I call it, "making your peace with the soul of the universe". So, I don't say that writing makes me happy. It's the other way around. If I don't write, I'll be very restless, and I won't be happy. So, I've been writing since I was a child. I started writing because I read literature very early on because we didn't have comics for some reason; my parents looked down at them, so our house was full of these big, big books that my uncle used to bring; he was studying his bachelor of arts, and my dad was a scientist, so there were a lot of journals. So what I grew up reading was science journals and beautiful literary works, like a lot of Russian literature. So I started writing very early on, and then it stopped when I went to med school. So I've been writing since **before I was born, I think. (laughs)**

Niv: Yeah. It's really easy. You just put a broom in the picture and then people are like, "Oh, she's trying to talk about the cleansing of the soul". No, it's a broom. (laughs). Abstract is really easy. I think artists have an open interpretation, unlike science fiction, right?

Tejas: Yeah

Niv: And so is poetry. I think people find art and poetry very safe spaces to be whatever they want and find a comfort of, like, someone else knowing them. So, I think that's why. Every artwork that I've created, I've had my own meaning behind it, like what I wanted to convey, but again, it's open to readers and people looking at the artwork how they want to interpret it, and I think that freedom is very intoxicating, comforting, and at times, therapeutic.

Tejas: So, when I was looking through both of your books, I saw that the first one was sort of based around your story and the second one was about people in general and about human rights.

Niv: I think the first poetry book I wrote was definitely after an event in my life. I was recovering from my heartbreak, and I had so much inside of me that was "breaking the dam". So that was what happened. So the first book was born out of this intense necessity of what I was experiencing, and also not just my personal experiences, but the experiences of others. And people would contact me and share their stories after they read my first book or if they had heard about me. So, yeah, my first book was about my words and my life, and the second book was shining the light on other people's stories and making them the heroes of their journeys.

Tejas: So, for your third book, how did you come up with the title the life currency?

Niv: You know, most of the things I have written are based off something I told someone. So, what I think happened was that I was in my apartment sitting with some friends. One of my friends brought their mother, who was going through some tough times, and I began to talk to her and comfort her. And I said, "You need to know where you're going to spend your life currency". And that was how I came up with that title. And that phrase really spoke to her. There are millions of words and phrases around the world, but only a few can click in one's head. I think that that phrase really connected with my friends. So, the book is about your life currency, about where to spend it, when to spend it, and who to spend it on.

Tejas: What is your main message throughout all of your poems and books?

Niv: I think that if I die tomorrow, I want to have some satisfaction that I did something to make a difference. I want to
pursue my purpose and my passion to help others in life. I think somewhere a word can help change someone's life forever. So that is what my message is, to fulfill your purpose on this Earth and to help your fellow humans. And even the simplest things like poetry can help make a difference.

Tejas: So that is all the questions I have for today, so thank you for your time.

Niv: Thank you Tejas!
Interview with Niv Lakhera at Niveditalakhera.com

The A List

Contents   page 15

The Art of Silence

Brenda Simmons, Poet & Advocate
Email: gmaweaponofpower@icloud.com

Like the paint brush of an artist the canvas of our mind can be created by beautiful bright illuminating colors. Like the bright yellow sunshine of joy and the purple bliss of soothing lavender. Or your mind can be plastered with ugly dark brown stains of splattered grime green and black spots. With haunting nightmares of memories of a tainted and tortured past.
How does one cope? Can we be healed from our past? Can we get to "worthy"? Do we cry out or do we remain in the silence of our pain?

Ok this is a heavy subject. But there definitely can be a phenomenal light at the end of a tumultuous tunnel, leading to a beginning of a new enlightenment. This takes work, encouraging support, and an unrelenting Will to Live Laugh and embrace Life.

Today the chirping of the beautiful AFRICAN birds is my solace today. My feet are a bit swollen from the long ride to our next destination here in Uganda, to the Rwakobo Resort. The profound sound of nature still brings a silence of surrender. No internet, no phone. At this serene resort place of surrender I discover its total source of energy is run by Solar. In Africa it was so amazing to see how resourceful they are out of pure necessity. And reflecting how wasteful we are.

And with limited and sporadic source of WIFI I return to pen in hand to journal in my black and white marble notebook. Seated in the back seat of the Jeep. We have a long two-hour journey to our next destination to Kampala. I look up from writing and I glance over to see my granddaughter somehow head into a sort of weird position but seemingly comfortably nodding out. I grab a sneak pic. She would be outraged to know I took a pic of her. Bad Gma. Bad Bad Gma.

I noticed my daughter who's seated upfront "co -pilot" with the driver, is also knocked out. On our way to Kampala, I look to the right and Michael (our driver/tour guide) announces "we are passing Lake Victoria". On the left miles and miles covered with structural greenery a pretty amazing sight. Michael shares all what you see is tea. Major export in Uganda.

Pen in hand I return to my black and white journal. The art of silence on our four-hour journey to Kampala is sometimes "un-silenced" by the announcement of important informative info followed by my many questions of the cultural surroundings. The journey continues in the art of silence, only sound is the rolling of the Jeep tired over the faint snoring.

Silence can be filled with an amazing quietness that's healing. Mind released from the rustle and bustle of thoughts of approaching deadlines, meetings, and setting up more meetings. The clamorous constant running in our minds can be as exhausting as running a marathon. A marathon that never seems to have a finish line. Ok have you ever met or know someone that their best bragging quality is a Vomiting vocabulary? They know everything about everything. If they are not in the conversation, they will rudely interrupt the conversation to find out "what ya talking bout". Or just butt in the conversation and completely change the topic to "whatever"!!! Leaving the other parties in the conversation starched with big eyed expressions.

Pleasantly smiling but Screaming inside "Shut the Hell Up". We all do it. We see them coming and we put our feet in fast gear. I've discovered that some people hate the art of silence. I ponder that perhaps in silence it forces them to hear thoughts of a devastating past. Or the familiar silent screaming of their voice of an attacking situation they try to forget. The repeating nightmare that won't be SILENCED. So much so that they must sleep with the tv on and a distant night light.

It's so much that can be gained by knowing the "Art of Silence". With peace of mind our eyes can see us through many avoidances and lead us to the path to our God ordained destiny. I embrace the art of silence. It does the Body good. The Soul and Mind folds their hands in solitude and peace.

With Perseverance Success is Assured!

Izuchukwu Raphael Onwusonye, Author

Email: tochionwusonye@gmail.com

"Great works are performed not by strength but by perseverance"   — Samuel Johnson.

Perseverance is steady persistence in a course of action, a purpose, a state especially in spite of difficulties, obstacles or discouragement.

Merriam Webster Dictionary defined perseverance as a continued effort to achieve something despite difficulties, failure or opposition.

Perseverance is not giving up. It is persistence and tenacity, the effort required to do something and keep doing it till the end, even if it's hard.

Perseverance originally comes from the Latin word perseverantia which means to abide by something strictly. This makes sense, because if you are doing something in spite of all the difficulty, you are being strict on yourself. Sailing around the world and climbing Mt Everest are acts requiring perseverance per say, even things like learning a new language require perseverance and daily practice. Investing the same energy in your business or work will keep you going through once you are persistent, success is assured.

People who persevere show steadfastness in doing something despite how hard it is or how long it takes to reach the goal. If you persevere, you can reach your goals by the grace of God.

Thomas Edison achieved great success through perseverance. He did not invent the light bulb on his first try; rather he put more than 6,000 substances to the test before he discovered that carbonized cotton thread makes a nice filament for the electric light bulb **"Genius is one percent inspiration and Ninety-nine percent perspiration".**

By remaining steadfast and determined in whatever it may be that you are desiring to see manifest in your life is of crucial importance if you are to bring about those results that you truly do desire, as we can see perseverance is an action that we must take, to remain steadfast in that action until the desired outcome is achieved.

It takes hard work and time to build up, it is a well-established fact that success is not achieved overnight; perseverance is the key to a successful life. If you keep persevering, long enough you will achieve your true potential. Just remind yourself that you can do anything you set your mind on, but it takes persistence, action and courage to face your fears.

One of Tom Hopkins favorite quote on perseverance

"I am not judged by the number of times I fail, but by the number of times I succeed and the number of times I succeed is in direct proportion to the number of times I fail and keep trying."

Perseverance means, to go on with that which you are doing no matter what you face and to remain steadfast in accomplishing the different task. Perseverance requires a higher level of patience. It doesn't matter what your goal is or how long it takes you to reach that goal. The chances of your success depend largely on your willingness to persist and persevere.

When you need to achieve a high level of success, perseverance is an essential element; it's a great tool to use and doesn't require any training. It comes naturally and requires a strong will and passion. Having passion for something will help you persist over doing something you like, and this will help you achieve success **"determination brings success"** as we rightly say or when advising people.

Have you ever wondered how some famous personalities achieved great heights of success? How did they stay positive despite failure? However, they kept on going, remained persistent, and their perseverance helped them to reach the peak of the mountain. Research has found that perseverance is a primary character strength linked to school achievement, productivity and success at work. Your perseverance keeps you engaged, focused and connected with what you are doing, perseverance is not only a strength to help you accomplish your goals and dreams, it is also your strength of engagement. Start taking full ownership of the goals you have set to achieve, you perceive to control your own fate, start thinking as a firm believer as if your destiny is in your hands.

 Although, failure at the start or beginning of the project or task can lead to frustration, and it shatters the self-confidence you had at the beginning and you might be considering giving up that goal or dreams because you once failed and you didn't feel you can ever succeed in life; wrong. Remember Stephen Grover Cleveland was an American politician and lawyer who was the 22nd and 24th President of the United States. Grover Cleveland was elected President (1884) and then lost his re-election campaign (1888) and came back again to win the presidency for a second time (1892).

 Similarly, just like Muhammadu Buhari, a current Nigerian politician, currently serving as the President of Nigeria, he unsuccessfully ran for the office of the President of Nigeria in the (2003), (2007) and (2011) general elections, but in December (2014), he emerged as the presidential candidate of the All Progressive Congress for the March (2015) general elections. Buhari won the election defeating the incumbent President Goodluck Jonathan and this marked the first time in the history of Nigeria that an incumbent President lost to an opposition candidate in a general election.

Success isn't a way, path or a straight line. It is a confused road with various ups and downs, and you should navigate it with popular care. You might fall or fail in the beginning or even get lost in your way. However, with perseverance, you will eventually reach your destination.

A person who practices perseverance is more trustworthy than the rest, because people know that you are not going to quit, no matter how hard the situation gets, and you will hold your ground.

 Many of life's failures are people who did not realize how close they were to success when they gave up"—Thomas Edison.

Staying rooted in the confidence that success is inevitable, if you continue to make a concerted effort to attain it. Because perseverance is the relentless attempt to achieve success and accomplish your desired goals. You can easily say "I CAN DO IT" but those who persevere don't just say it, they do it and they live in it never giving up. You achieve not simply by trying, but by persevering.

 'Don't be discouraged. It's often the last key in the bunch that opens the lock'

Perseverance will give you the power, never let the obstacles in your way block you from where you want to go or what you want to achieve in life. Keep your mind focused and consistent, success is assured.

You may encounter many defeats, but you must not be defeated. Life has its ups and downs. Learning to get through the downs is the key to being successful. Always remember that without challenges, struggles and obstacles, life wouldn't make much sense. **"What cannot kill you will only make you stronger".** You become stronger, more grateful when you strongly believe in your capacity to persevere.

"Most of the important things in the world have been accomplished by people who have kept on trying when there seemed to be no hope at all – Dale Carnegie

No matter the area your goals in life have to do with, if you persevere, you will succeed. The key to success is to continue making efforts to achieve your goal even if you failed on the first attempt. The path to success is heavily spotted with obstacles, but your ability to persevere improves your odds of winning. The world you desire can be won.

You cannot achieve anything without action. Action is what makes your dreams come true. It is also action that translates plans into tangible results or goal oriented. Thinking and planning alone won't cut it, sustained action is what separates winners from losers.

"I have not failed; I have just found 10,000 ways that won't work" – Thomas A Edison

Don't forget to celebrate your small wins and mini achievements along the way, forgive yourself for failing, learn from your mistakes, and adjust course accordingly. But never give up. Besides you can always call on coaches, mentors, priests and others to assist you in taking better care of yourself. You need to put in the necessary efforts and resources to succeed in life.

Jennene Christine
Obremski